# CHRISTMAS
# 2000
## stickers
### Frosty, festive, and fun!

PaRragon

Bath · New York · Cologne · Melbourne · Delhi
Hong Kong · Shenzhen · Singapore · Amsterdam

# Toy-rific Workshop!

These little elves are the best toymakers in town!
Fill the workshop with more busy elves and fantastic toys.

Color in the pile of presents.

READY FOR SLEIGH

# Christmas Chaos

Help Santa find his missing sack of presents in time for Christmas Eve!

# Teddy Time

Give these giant teddy bears smiley faces and fluffy fur.

# Festive Foods

Follow the lines to help everyone reach their favorite festive treat.

Answer: A2, B3, C1.

# What's Missing?

Join the dots to find out what is missing from Santa's head.

What would you like me to bring you this year?

# Wonderful Wish List

Draw or write what you would like for Christmas!

# Frosty Fishing!

These elves are having some ice fishing fun.
Add more fish swimming in the watery wonderland.

# Merry Matching

Match each cheerful child with their favorite toy.

A    B    C    D    E

1    2    3    4    5

# Christmas Counting

How many sparkly angels?

How many beautiful baubles?

How many yummy candy canes?

# I Spy in the Snow!

Help the rabbit find the reindeer! Then color the reindeer so Santa can see them.

# Christmas Decorating!

The tree is up, the fire is flickering ... but someone forgot the decorations! Add some Christmas spirit to this room.

# Snack Time for Santa

Yum! Santa loves Christmassy treats!
Draw what you think he likes to eat.

# Festive Forgetfulness

Follow the lines to find out what this forgetful elf
has left in the toy workshop.

It must be
around here
somewhere!

# Merry Matching

One of these Christmas stars is different from the rest.
Circle the one that's not like the others.

A        B        C        D        E

# Snowball Fight!

Watch out! Snowballs are flying at the North Pole today!
Join in the fun by adding more playful elves
and swooshing snowballs.

Gotcha!

# Meeting Santa!

Find and circle six differences between these two pictures of super-excited children.

# A-maze-ing Wrapping Paper

Help this elf reach the wrapping paper to bring to Santa's sleigh.

# Toymaking Mishaps

Circle the one that is different in each group.

# Relaxing Reindeer

After a long night of delivering presents, it's time for these hungry reindeer to have a rest.
Fill their food bowls with crunchy carrots and add more reindeer friends.

DASHER     DANCER     PRANCER     RUDOLPH     VIXEN

Find and circle Holly the cat.
(She has a red collar.)

COMET     CUPID     DONNER     BLITZEN

Oh deer ...

Answer: Holly the cat is sipping milk by Blitzen's stable.

# Where's Rudolph?

Can you find Rudolph in this Christmassy crowd?

Answer: Rudolph is hiding behind a tree.

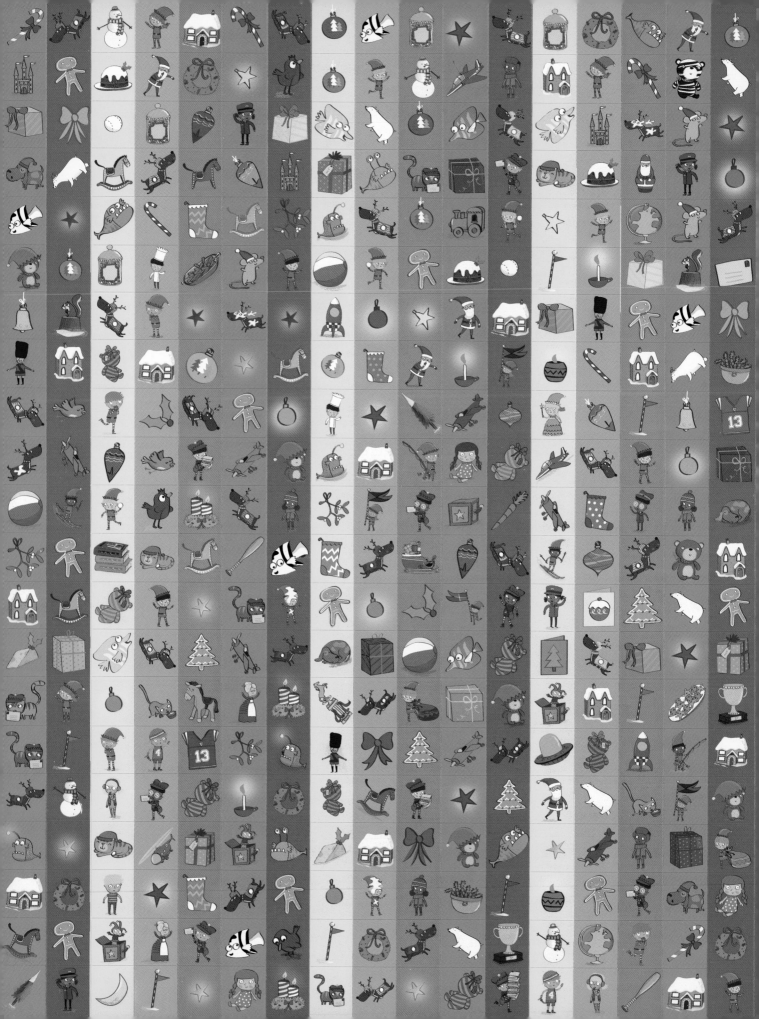

# Pretty Paper

Make these presents look festive!
Color in the wrapping paper with
fun patterns and bright colors.

# Perfect Presents

What do these presents look like unwrapped? Draw a line to join each pair.

1    2    3    4

A    B    C    D

# Jolly Christmas Party!

Grab your party hat and dancing shoes ... It's time for Santa's Christmas party!
Join in the celebration by adding more partying elves.

# Where Are My Wings?

Join the dots to help this Christmas angel fly through the festive sky.

2   1   1   2
3           3
10   10
9       9
4           4
5   8         8   5
6           6
7           7

# Christmas Cookies!

Which comes next, a gingerbread man or a gingerbread tree?
Draw the next tasty treat in the box.

# Tricky Tree

Uh-oh! These elves are in trouble! Quickly trace the star on top of the tree to fix it in place, so that the elves can climb down to safety.

How many elves are there? Write the number here.

# Midnight Dash

Do you hear bells jingling? Santa and his sleigh are soaring through the clouds. Fill the sky with twinkling stars to help light the way!

Ho, ho, ho!

Add more presents to the sleigh!

Add more snow-covered houses!

# Present Surprise

Draw your favorite toys inside these Christmas presents.

# Season's Greetings

Oops—someone in this picture doesn't belong!
Circle the one who doesn't belong.

Answer: The Easter bunny doesn't belong.

# Elf Academy

Even elves go to school, and Mrs. Claus is a terrific teacher! What are the elves learning today?

Trace over the words on the whiteboard to find out.

How to wrap a present

This is harder than the elf-abet!

# Mistletoe Mountain

Zoooom! The North Pole has some of the best ski slopes around! Add more elves with a need for speed.

Draw hats on the elves to keep them warm!

# Jingle All the Way!

Find and circle six differences between these two groups of carol singers.

# Santa's Suit

Santa can't deliver presents in his underwear! Use your stickers to dress Santa in his suit.

# Decorate the Tree

Doodle and color to turn this plain tree into the perfect festive decoration.

Add some candy canes, lights, and brightly colored baubles!

# Christmas Dinner

You'd better be hungry—it's time for turkey and all the trimmings! Add some yummy Christmas food to the table.

Mmmm!

Purrrrr!

Find and circle a sneaky little mouse.

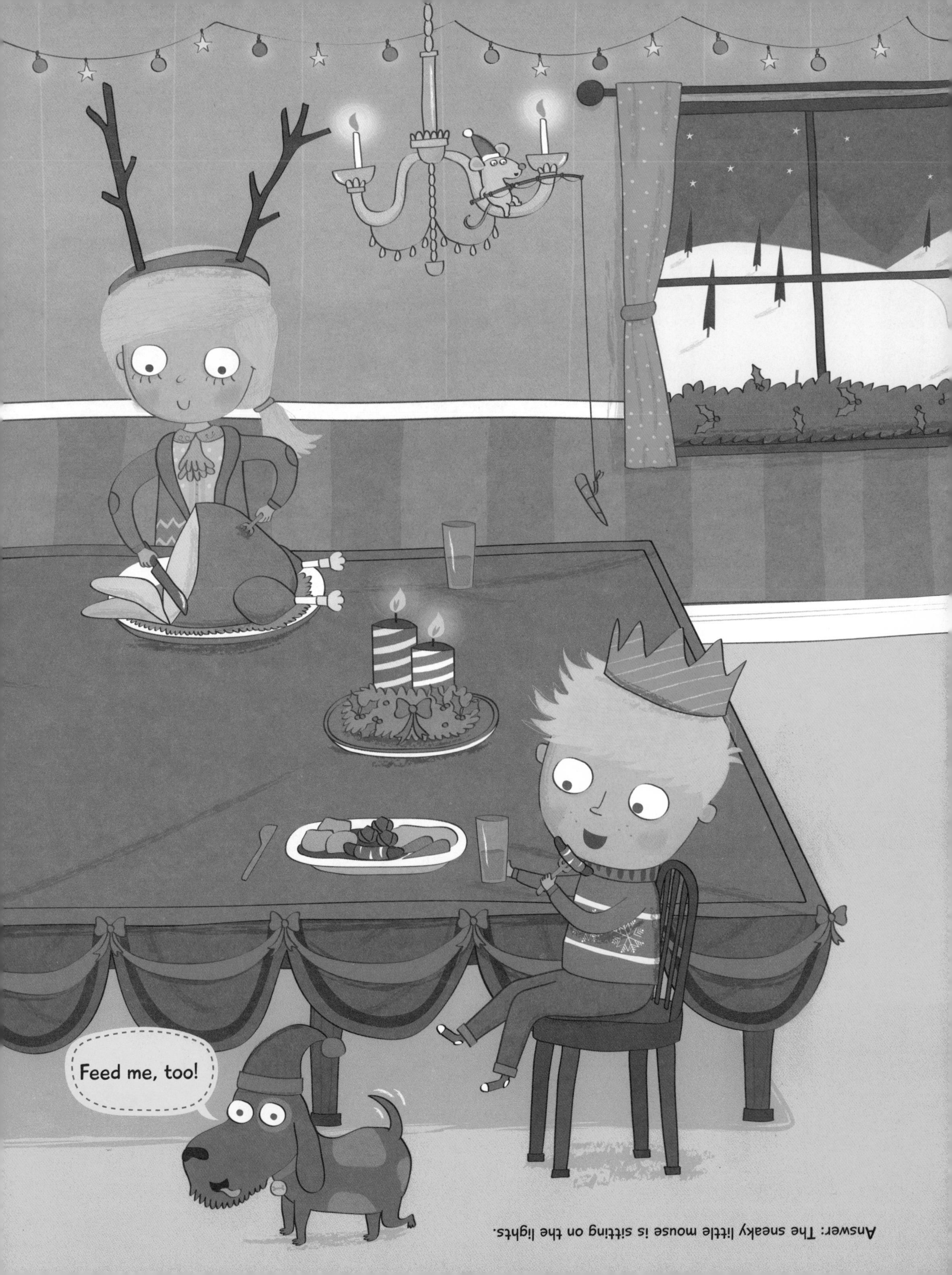


Answer: The sneaky little mouse is sitting on the lights.

# Santa's Portrait

**1** Draw a face with a bushy beard!

**2** Doodle his body with a big belly and a belt.

**3** Add some legs and boots.

**4** Finish with the hat!

Follow the steps and draw your own Santa here.

# Christmas Knitting

Mrs. Claus is knitting something for every elf at the North Pole!
Color in the clothes with your best Christmassy colors.

# Reindeer in the Snow

Grumble ...

Which line leads this soggy reindeer
back to the dry stables?

Toy Workshop

Santa's House

Reindeer Stables

A  B  C

Answer: Line B leads to the stables.

# North Pole Post Office

Take a sneak peek into Santa's merry mailroom! Fill it with more elves to help sort the letters from boys and girls all over the world.

# Cozy Christmas

Find and circle five differences between these two festive fireplaces.

Answers: The cat has been replaced by a dog, the green stocking is missing, one of the cards has changed, a candle is missing, the ribbon decoration has changed.

# Chimney Challenge

Santa has a busy night ahead! Count the chimneys and write the number in the cloud.

I ho-ho-hope I fit!

Answer: There are 7 chimneys.

# Decorated Dot-to-Dot

Join the dots to make something tall, green, and Christmassy!
Then doodle some decorations.

14    1

13    12        3    2

11    10              5    4

9              8    7              6

# Sweet Dreams for Santa

Shhh! Santa is downstairs delivering presents, while these sleepy children are tucked up in bed! What gifts do you think they are dreaming of?

# Christmas Codebreaker

Crack the code to find out what Santa is saying!

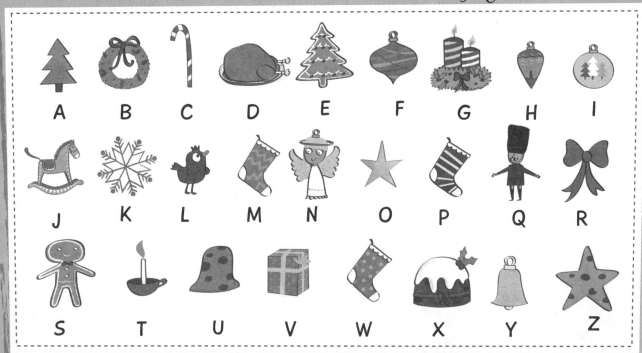